illions of Americans remember Dick and Jane (and Sally and Spot too!). The little stories with their simple vocabulary words and warmly rendered illustrations were a hallmark of American education in the 1950s and 1960s.

But the first Dick and Jane stories actually appeared much earlier—in the Scott Foresman Elson Basic Reader Pre-Primer, copyright 1930. These books featured short, upbeat, and highly readable stories for children. The pages were filled with colorful characters and large, easy-to-read Century Schoolbook typeface. There were fun adventures around every corner of Dick and Jane's world.

Generations of American children learned to read with Dick and Jane, and many still cherish the memory of reading the simple stories on their own. Today, Pearson Scott Foresman remains committed to helping all children learn to read—and love to read. As part of Pearson Education, the world's largest educational publisher, Pearson Scott Foresman is honored to reissue these classic Dick and Jane stories, with Grosset & Dunlap, a division of Penguin Young Readers Group. Reading has always been at the heart of everything we do, and we sincerely hope that reading is an important part of your life too.

Dick and Jane is a registered trademark of Addison-Wesley Educational Publishers, Inc.
From GUESS WHO. Copyright © 1951 by Scott, Foresman and Company, copyright
renewed 1979. From THE NEW WE COME AND GO. Copyright © 1956 by Scott, Foresman
and Company, copyright renewed 1984. All rights reserved. Published in 2004 by Grosset &
Dunlap, a division of Penguin Young Readers Group, 345 Hudson Street, New York, NY,
10014. GROSSET & DUNLAP is a trademark of Penguin Group (USA) Inc. Published
simultaneously in Canada. Printed in the U.S.A.

Library of Congress Cataloging-in-Publication Data
Who can help?
    p. cm. — (Read with Dick and Jane ; 8)
    Summary: A collection of classic Dick and Jane stories in which they give and receive help
while spending time with Sally, Tim, Spot, Puff, and their parents.
    ISBN 0-448-43407-5 (pbk.) — ISBN 0-448-43493-8 (hardcover)
    [1. Helpfulness—Fiction. 2. Play—Fiction. 3. Pets—Fiction. 4. Vocabulary.] I. Series.
PZ7.W6197 2004
[E]—dc22   2003016828

ISBN 0-448-43493-8 (GB)   A B C D E F G H I J
ISBN 0-448-43407-5 (pbk)   A B C D E F G H I J

Read with

Dick and Jane

Who Can Help?

GROSSET & DUNLAP • NEW YORK

Find Dick

Jane said, "I see you.

I see you, Sally.

I can find you.

I can not find Dick.

Help me, Sally.

Help me find Dick."

Jane said, "Oh, Father.
I can not find Dick.
And we can not play.
Help me, Father.
Help me find Dick."

Father said, "Look, Jane.
Look, look, look.
You can find Dick."

Sally said, "Oh, oh.
I see Dick now.
Father and I see Dick.
We see funny Dick.
Look, Jane, look.
You can find Dick now."

Who Can Help?

Dick said, "Mother, Mother.
Come here.
I want you.
Come and help me.

Oh, Jane.
Oh, Father.
Who can come?
Who can come and help me?"

Dick said, "Go away, Spot.

You can not help me.

Oh, my.

Oh, my.

I want Mother.

Mother can help me.

Run, Spot, run.

Run and find Mother."

Dick said, "Oh, Spot.
Now I can come in.
You can help me.
Little Spot can help.
You can help me come in."

See What I See

Dick said, "Look, Sally.

Look down here.

See what I see.

See my big cookie.

See me and my big cookie.

You can see Spot here.

Spot wants my big cookie."

"Oh, oh," said Sally.
"I see Tim and me.
And now I see Puff.
Puff is in here.
I see little Puff.
Puff and Tim and me."

Sally said, "Look, Jane.
Look down here.
You can see Jane in here."

Jane said, "Oh, oh, oh.
Who sees what I see?
It is something funny.
It is not Jane."

Little Boat

Sally said, "See my boat.

I want my little boat.

I want my little boat in here."

Jane said, "Dick can get it.

Dick is big.

Dick can go and get it."

"Not now," said Dick.

"I can not get it now."

Jane said, "Come, Sally.
Come and play.
Here is Tim."

"I want my boat," said Sally.
"Who can get it for me?
Is Father here?
Father can get it for me."

Sally said, "Oh, oh, oh.

Come here, Dick.

See what I see.

See my little blue boat now.

See who wants my boat.

My little blue boat.

See who wants it now."

What Can Dick Make?

Jane said, "Look, Sally.
See what I can make.
It is big and yellow.
It is for Puff."

Sally said, "Look, Mother.
I can make something for Tim.
Jane can make something for Puff.
What can Dick make?"

Dick said, "I can make something.
Come and see what it is."

"Is it blue?" said Sally.
"Is it yellow?
Is it red?"

Dick said, "Oh, my.
It is red and yellow and blue.
Come and see what it is."

Jane said, "Look, Sally.
Dick can make something pretty.
See what Dick can make."

"I see it," said Sally.
"It is pretty.
What is it?"

Jane said. "Oh, Sally.
It is Dick."

See It Go

Father said, "Look in here.
You can find something.
Something you want."

Dick said, "Look, Jane, look.
Red, yellow, and blue.
Yellow is for me.
Who wants red and blue?"

Jane said, "I want blue.
Red is for Sally."

Dick said, "Come, Sally.
Come and get something.
Red for you and blue for Jane."

Sally said, "Oh, Dick.
Pretty, pretty.
Make it big.
Make it big, big, big."

Jane said, "Run, Spot.
Run away, Puff.
See what I see.
Run, run, run."

"Now look," said Dick.

"See my boat.

See my boat go.

I can make it go away.

See it go.

Oh, see it go."

Little Tim Can Help

Dick said, "Look, look.
Here we come.
We can help."

Jane said, "Run, Dick.
Run, run.
We can help."

"Look here," said Sally.

"One is for Dick.

One is for Jane.

And one is for Baby Sally."

"Look, Mother," said Sally.

"Here we come.

See little Tim.

Tim can help.

Tim can help Mother.

Oh, oh.

Tim is funny."

JE READ
Read with Dick and Jane
Who can help?

$13.89

DATE			